Green Auricula

A FLORAL CALENDAR

Also by Marie Angel:

Catscript
Cottage Flowers
Painting for Calligraphers

Bird, Beast and Flowers *(Chatto and Windus)*
The Art of Calligraphy *(Robert Hale)*

illustrations for:
The Tale of Tuppenny by Beatrix Potter *(Warne)*
The Tale of the Faithful Dove by Beatrix Potter *(Warne)*

Marie Angel
A FLORAL CALENDAR
and other flower lore

Pelham Books

First published in Great Britain by
Pelham Books Ltd
44 Bedford Square
London WC1B 3DP
1985

Angel, Marie
A floral calendar : and other flower lore.
1. Symbolism of flowers—Pictorial works
I. Title
398'.368213'0222   GR780

ISBN 0-7207-1610-1

Printed and bound in Holland by
L Van Leer and Co Ltd, Deventer

Contents

Geranium   phaeum

For
Charles and Elizabeth Pizzey
and Jean de Courville

Introduction

In the Western World, up to the end of the Middle Ages, the prime interest in flowers and plants was not for their beauty or decorative power, but for their usefulness as food and medicines. Monasteries were particularly associated with the medicinal use of plants, and it would seem appropriate, therefore, that the names of the flowers they cultivated so assiduously should be given to the hours of the canonical day (page 22).

The first Floral Calendar given here (pages 9-21) also owes much of its composition to monks or other religious, since it is derived from the Catholic Calendar of Saints' Feast Days, each flower or plant being the emblem of a particular saint.

The most ancient of the three floral calendars illustrated here is the Chinese (pages 70-71); originally the flowers were attributes of certain deities worshipped at particular seasons of the year. This calendar includes plants which have become favourites in Western gardens, such as the magnificent tree peonies, the exotic gardenia, and the decorative chrysanthemum and poppy.

The Japanese Calendar also has a religious background. The autumn Nanakusa named in the Calendar (pages 72-3) consists of seven different flowers which bloom during October when the Festival of the Full Moon is celebrated by decorating the house with the Seven Grasses of Autumn. These include the pink *(Dianthus superbus)*, the purple balloon flower *(Platycodon grandiflorum)*, the coloured large convolvulus *(Ipomoea hederacea)* and a variegated grass with silver panicles *(Eulalia japonica)*.

Symbolic meanings were given to plants from the earliest times, but the Language of Flowers popularised in Victorian England was introduced by Lady Mary Wortley Montagu who noted in Constantinople that it was the custom of Turkish women to send messages using flowers which would have a meaning for the recipient. The portrait of the little Victorian child preceding it here (on page 24) has a flower border of daisies (innocence), primroses (early youth and sadness) and blue periwinkles (early friendship).

The 'flower clocks' illustrated on pages 66 and 67 are based on Linnaeus's, the great eighteenth-century Swedish botanist, famous 'Watch of Flora' at Uppsala. Flower horologes are of great antiquity (one is mentioned in the writings of Pliny, for example), and were often in the sixteenth and seventeenth centuries planted out in small beds in front of sundials with figures fashioned out of box. To supplement Linnaeus's list, some of the plants have been taken from the list given in *The Language of Flowers* by Mrs L. Burke.

For the hours of eleven, twelve, one and two on the opening dial no flowers were given in either list; to make the dial more complete the spaces have been filled with night-flowering plants in the following order: tobacco plant, evening primrose, night-scented stock and night-flowering campion.

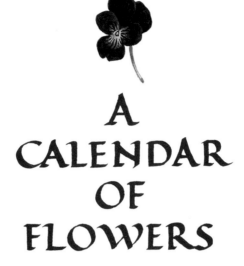

A
CALENDAR
OF
FLOWERS

1	Laurustinus	Garden Anemone	17
2	Groundsel	Four-toothed Moss	18
3	Persian Iris	White Dead Nettle	19
4	Hazel	Woolly Dead Nettle	20
5	Hellebore	Black Hellebore	21
6	Screw Moss	Whitlow Grass	22
7	Portugese Laurel	Peziza	23
8	Yellow Tremella	Stalkless Moss	24
9	Laurel	Winter Hellebore	25
10	Gorse or Furze	Coltsfoot	26
11	Early Moss	Earth Moss	27
12	Moss	Double Daisy	28
13	Common Yew	Flowering Fern	29
14	Barren Strawberry	Spleenwort	30
15	Ivy	Hart's-tongue	31
16	Red Dead Nettle		

JANUARY

1	Bay Tree	Scotch Crocus	17
2	Snowdrop	Wall Speedwell	18
3	Water Moss	Field Speedwell	19
4	Goldilocks	Blue-eyes	20
5	Primrose	White Crocus	21
6	Blue Hyacinth	Herb Margaret	22
7	Cyclamen	Apricot-blossom	23
8	Hair Moss	Great Fern	24
9	Roman Narcissus	Peach-blossom	25
10	Mezereon	Lesser Periwinkle	26
11	Red Primrose	Lungwort	27
12	Anemone	Purple Crocus	28
13	Polyanthus	Purple-striped	29
14	Yellow Crocus	Crocus	
15	Golden Crocus		
16	Lilac Primrose		

FEBRUARY

1	Leek	Shamrock
2	Chickweed (Mouse-eared)	Leopard's Bane (Great)
3	Golden Fig	Star of Bethlehem
4	Chickweed (Common)	Dog's Violet
5	Green Hellebore	Corydalis
6	Lent Lily	Celandine
7	Early Daffodil	Peerless Daffodil
8	Great Jonquil	Golden Saxifrage
9	Daffodil	Marygold
10	Chickweed (upright)	Henbane
11	Cornish Heath	Sweet Jonquil
12	Ixia	Leopard's Bane
13	Heart's-ease	Oxlip
14	Alpine Bindweed	Watercress
15	Common Coltsfoot	Benjamin-tree
16	Sweet Violet	

MARCH

1 Dog's Mercury	17 Broad-leaved Arum
2 White Violet	18 Musk Narcissus
3 Evergreen Alkanet	19 Garlic
4 Crown Imperial (Red)	20 Spring Snowflake
5 Crown Imperial (Yellow)	21 Cypress Narcissus
6 Hyacinth	22 Wood Crowfoot
7 Wood Anemone	23 Harebell
8 Ground Ivy	24 Blackthorn
9 Red Polyanthus	25 Clarimond Tulip
10 Pale Violet	26 Yellow Erysimon
11 Dandelion	27 Great Daffodil
12 Saxifrage	28 Spotted Arum
13 Green Narcissus	29 Herb Robert
14 Common Borage	30 Cowslip
15 Greater Stitchwort	
16 Yellow Tulip	

APRIL

1	Bachelor's Button	17	Early Red Poppy
2	Charlock	18	Hawkweed
3	Poetic Narcissus	19	Monkshood
4	Stock Gillyflower	20	Horse Chestnut
5	Apple-blossom	21	Ragged Robin
6	Globe Flower	22	Star of Bethlehem
7	Globe Flower (Asiatic)	23	Lilac
8	Lily of the Valley	24	Monkey Poppy
9	Lily of the Valley	25	Herb Bennet
10	Peony (Slender-leaved)	26	Yellow Azalea
11	Asphodel	27	Buttercup
12	German Iris	28	Lurid Iris
13	Common Comfrey	29	Bluebottle
14	Common Peony	30	Spearwort
15	Welsh Poppy	31	Yellow Turk's-cap
16	Star of Bethlehem		Lily

MAY

1	Yellow Rose	Monkey Flower (Yellow)	17
2	Common Pimpernel	Horned Poppy	18
3	Rose of Meaux	La Julienne de Nuit	19
4	Indian Pink	Doubtful Poppy	20
5	China Rose	Viper's Bugloss	21
6	Common Pink	Canterbury Bell	22
7	Red Centaury	Ladies' Slipper	23
8	Moneywort	St. John's Wort	24
9	Barberry	Sweet William	25
10	Bright Yellow Iris	Alpine Sowthistle	26
11	Midsummer Daisy	St. John's Wort (Perforate)	27
12	White Dog Rose	Blue Cornflower	28
13	Garden Ranunculus	Yellow Rattle	29
14	Sweet Basil	Yellow Cistus	30
15	Sensitive Plant		
16	Moss Rose		

JUNE

1 Agrimony	Sweet Pea 17
2 White Lily	Autumn Marygold 18
3 Common Mallow	Golden Hawkweed 19
4 Tawny Day Lily	Dragon's-head (Virginian) 20
5 Double Yellow Rose	Philadelphian Lily 21
6 Hawkweed	African Lily 22
7 Nasturtium	Musk Flower 23
8 Evening Primrose	Lupine Tree 24
9 Marsh Sowthistle	Herb Christopher 25
10 Speckled Snapdragon	Chamomile 26
11 Yellow Lupine	Loosestrife 27
12 Great Snapdragon	Mountain Groundsel 28
13 Blue Lupine	Red Chironia 29
14 Red Lupine	White Mullein 30
15 Cape Marygold	Yellow Mullein 31
16 Convolvulus	

JULY

1. Thorn Apple
2. Tiger Lily
3. Hollyhock (Egyptian)
4. Bluebell
5. Water Lily
6. Meadow Saffron
7. Amaranth (Common)
8. Love-lies-bleeding
9. Yellow Ragwort
10. Balsam
11. China Aster
12. Corn Sowthistle
13. Groundsel (Marsh)
14. Zinnia
15. Virgin's Bower
16. Belladonna Lily
17. Snapdragon
18. African Marigold
19. Cat's-tail Grass
20. Dandelion
21. French Marigold
22. Timothy Grass
23. Common Tansy
24. Tall Sunflower
25. Perennial Sunflower
26. Amaryllis (Banded)
27. Hedge Hawkweed
28. Golden Rod
29. Yellow Hollyhock
30. Guernsey Lily
31. Pheasant's Eye

AUGUST

1	Orpine	Mallow (Narrow-leaved)	17
2	Golden Rod	Pendulous Starwort	18
3	Common Fleabane	Devil's-bit Scabious	19
4	Pink Soapwort	Meadow Saffron (Common)	20
5	Mushroom	Passion Flower (Fringed-leaved)	21
6	Dandelion	Boletus-tree	22
7	Golden Starwort	White Starwort	23
8	Blue Starwort	Fungus	24
9	Golden Rod (Canadian)	Great Boletus	25
10	Autumnal Crocus	Golden Rod (Great)	26
11	Meadow Saffron (Variegated)	White Starwort (small-leaved)	27
12	Passion Flower	Golden Rod (Great)	28
13	Officinal Crocus	Michaelmas Daisy	29
14	Passion Flower (Blue)	Golden Amaryllis	30
15	Byzantine Saffron		
16	Sea-blue Starwort		

SEPTEMBER

1 Lowly Amaryllis	Dwarf Sunflower 17
2 Soapwort	Mushroom 18
3 Downy Helenium	Thickseed 19
4 Southernwood	Sweet Sultan (Yellow) 20
5 Chamomile(Star-like)	Silphium 21
6 Feverfew (creeping)	Starwort(Slender-stalked) 22
7 Chrysanthemum	Silphium(Rough leaved) 23
8 Sweet Maudlin	Starwort (Carolina) 24
9 Milky Mushroom	Starwort (Fleabane) 25
10 Cape Aletris	Golden Rod(Late flowering 26
11 Common Holly	Starwort (Floribund) 27
12 Wavy Fleabane	Chrysanthemum 28
13 Yellow Helenium	Narcissus(Green Autumnal) 29
14 Indian Fleabane	Mixen Mushroom 30
15 Sweet Sultan	Thickseed 31
16 Yarrow	

OCTOBER

1	Laurustinus	Thorn Apple	17
2	Winter Cherry	Passion Flower (notch leafed)	18
3	Primrose	Passion Flower (apple-fruited)	19
4	Arbutus	Stapelia (Red)	20
5	Winter Cherry	Wood Sorrel	21
6	Yew	Wood Sorrel (tube flowered)	22
7	Furcroa	Sorrel (convex)	23
8	Cape Aletris	Stapelia (starry)	24
9	Aletris (Glaucous-leaved)	Sweet Butterbur	25
10	Scots Fir	Sorrel (Linnear)	26
11	Weymouth Pine	Sorrel (Lupine-leaved)	27
12	Aloe (orange-flowering)	Stapelia (variegated)	28
13	Bay	Sphenogyne	29
14	Portugese Laurel	Sorrel (tricolor)	30
15	Coltsfoot		
16	African Hemp		

NOVEMBER

1	Stapelia	White Cedar	17
2	Lemon Geodurum	New Holland Cypress	18
3	Indian-tree	Bicolor Heath	19
4	Gooseberry (Barbadoes)	Stone Pine	20
5	Hibiscus (long-stalked)	Sparrow-wort	21
6	Heath (nest-flowered)	Pellucid Heath	22
7	Hairy Achania	Cedar of Lebanon	23
8	Arbor Vitae (American)	Frankincense Pine	24
9	Corsican Spruce	Holly	25
10	Portugal Cypress	Purple Heath	26
11	Aleppo Pine	Flame Heath	27
12	Ground Heath	Heath (blood-coloured)	28
13	Arbor Vitae (African)	Heath	29
14	Swamp Pine	Ponthieva	30
15	Pitch Pine	Winter Jasmine	31
16	Arbor Vitae (Chinese)		

DECEMBER

MEDIAEVAL HOURS

First Hour	Budding Roses
Second Hour	Heliotrope
Third Hour	White Roses
Fourth Hour	Hyacinths
Fifth Hour	Lemons
Sixth Hour	Lotus Blossom
Seventh Hour	Lupins
Eighth Hour	Oranges
Ninth Hour	Olive Leaves
Tenth Hour	Poplar Leaves
Eleventh Hour	Marigolds
Twelfth Hour	Pansies and Violets

THE
LANGUAGE
OF
FLOWERS

A

Abecedary	Volubility
Abatina	Fickleness
Acacia	Friendship
Acacia, Rose or White	Elegance
Acacia, Yellow	Secret love
Acanthus	The fine arts: Artifice
Acalia	Temperance
Achillea millifolia	War
Aconite (Wolfsbane)	Misanthropy
Aconite, Crowfoot	Lustre
Adonis, Flos	Painful recollections
African Marigold	Vulgar minds
Agnus Castus	Coldness: Indifference
Agrimony	Thankfulness
Almond, Common	Stupidity: Indiscretion
Almond, Flowering	Hope
Almond, Laurel	Perfidy
Allspice	Compassion
Aloe	Grief

Althæa Frutex	Persuasion
Alyssum, Sweet	Worth beyond beauty
Amaranth, Golbe	Immortality
	Unfading love
Amaranth, Cockscomb	Affectation
Amaryllis	Pride: Timidity
	Splendid beauty
Ambrosia	Love returned
American Cowslip	Divine beauty
American Elm	Patriotism
American Linden	Matrimony
American Starwort	Cheerfulness in old age
Amethyst	Admiration
Anemone, Wild	Sickness: Expectation
Anemone, Garden	Forsaken
Angelica	Inspiration
Angrec	Royalty
Apple	Temptation
Apple, Thorn	Deceitful charms

Apple, Blossom	Preference: Fame speaks him great & good
Apocynum, Dogsbane	Deceit
Arbor Vitae	Unchanging friendship Live for me
Arum, Wake Robin	Ardour
Ash-leaved Trumpet Flower	Separation
Ash Tree	Grandeur
Aspen Tree	Lamentation
Aster, China	Variety: Afterthought
Asphodel	My regrets follow you to the grave
Auricula	Painting
Auricula, Scarlet	Avarice
Austurtium	Splendour
Azalea	Temperance

Bachelor's Buttons	Celibacy
Balm	Sympathy
Balm, Gentle	Pleasantry
Balm of Gilead	Cure: Relief
Balsam, Red	Touch-me-not
	Impatient resolves
Balsam, Yellow	Impatience
Barberry	Sourness of temper
Barberry Tree	Sharpness
Basil	Hatred
Bay Leaf	I change but in
Bay (Rose)	death
Rhododendron	Danger: Beware
Bay Tree	Glory
Bay Wreath	Reward of merit
Bearded Crepis	Protection
Beech Tree	Prosperity
Bee Ophrys	Error
Bee Orchis	Industry

Belladonna	Silence
Bell Flower (Pyramidal)	Constancy
Bell Flower (small white)	Gratitude
Belvedere	I declare against you
Betony	Surprise
Bilberry	Treachery
Bindweed, Great	Insinuation
Bindweed, Small	Humility
Birch	Meekness
Bird's foot Trefoil	Revenge
Bittersweet	Truth
Black Poplar	Courage
Blackthorn	Difficulty
Bladder Nut Tree	Frivolity: Amusement
Bluebottle (Centaury)	Delicacy
Bluebell	Constancy
Blue-flowered Greek Valerian	Rupture
Bonus Henricus	Goodness

Borage	Bluntness
Box Tree	Stoicism
Bramble	Lowliness : Envy : Remorse
Branch of Currants	You please all
Branch of Thorns	Severity : Rigour
Bridal Rose	Happy love
Broom	Humility : Neatness
Buckbean	Calm : Repose
Bud of White Rose	Heart ignorant of love
Bugloss	Falsehood
Bulrush	Indiscretion : Docility
Bundle of Reeds with their Panicles	Music
Burdock	Importunity : Touch me not
Buttercup (Ringcup)	Ingratitude : Childishness
Butterfly Orchis	Gaiety
Butterfly Weed	Let me go

Cabbage	Profit
Cacalia	Adulation
Cactus	Warmth
Calla Aethiopica	Magnificent Beauty
Calycanthus	Benevolence
Camellia Japonica Red	Unpretending excellence
Camellia Japonica White	Perfected loveliness
Camomile	Energy in adversity
Canary Grass	Perseverance
Candytuft	Indifference
Canterbury Bell	Acknowledgment
Cape Jasmine	I'm too happy
Cardamine	Paternal error
Carnation, Deep Red	Alas! for my poor heart
Carnation, Striped	Refusal
Carnation, Yellow	Disdain
Cardinal Flower	Distinction

Catchfly	Snare
Catchfly, Red	Youthful love
Catchfly, White	Betrayed
Cedar	Strength
Cedar of Lebanon	Incorruptible
Cedar leaf	I live for thee
Celandine, Lesser	Joys to come
Centaury	Delicacy
Cereus, Creeping	Modest genius
Champignon	Suspicion
Chequered Fritillary	Persecution
Cherry Tree	Good education
Cherry Tree, White	Deception
Chestnut Tree	Do me justice: Luxury
Chickweed	Rendezvous
Chicory	Frugality
China Aster	Variety
China Aster, Double	I partake your sentiments
China Aster, Single	I will think of it

China Rose	Beauty always new
Chinese Chrysanthemum	Cheerfulness under adversity
Christmas Rose	Relieve my anxiety
Chrysanthemum, Red	I love
Chrysanthemum, White	Truth
Chrysanthemum, Yellow	Slighted love
Cinquefoil	Maternal affection
Circœa	Spell
Cistus or Rock Rose	Popular favour
Cistus, Gum	I shall die tomorrow
Citron	Ill-natured beauty
Clematis	Mental beauty
Clematis, Evergreen	Poverty
Clotbur	Rudeness: Pertinacity
Cloves	Dignity
Clover, Four-leaved	Be mine
Clover, Red	Industry
Clover, White	Think of me
Cobœa	Gossip

Cedar of Lebanon

Cockscomb, Amaranth	Foppery: Affectation
Colchicum	My best days are past
Coltsfoot	Justice shall be done
Columbine	Folly
Columbine, Purple	Resolved to win
Columbine, Red	Anxious and trembling
Convolvulus	Bonds
Convolvulus, Blue	Repose: Night
Convolvulus, Major	Extinguished hopes
Corchorus	Impatient of absence
Coreopsis	Always cheerful
Coreopsis Arkansa	Love at first sight
Coriander	Hidden worth
Corn	Riches
Corn, Broken	Quarrel
Corn Straw	Agreement
Corn Bottle	Delicacy
Corn Cockle	Gentility
Cornel Tree	Duration

Cypress

Coronella	Success crown your wishes
Cowslip	Pensiveness
Cowslip, American	Divine beauty: You are my divinity
Cranberry	Cure for heartache
Cress	Stability: Power
Crocus	Abuse not
Crocus, Spring	Youthful gladness
Crocus, Saffron	Mirth
Crown Imperial	Majesty: Power
Crows bill	Envy
Crowfoot	Ingratitude
Crowfoot, Aconite-leaved	Lustre
Cuckoo Plant	Ardour
Cudweed, American	Unceasing remembrance
Currant	Thy frown will kill me
Cuscuta	Meanness
Cyclamen	Diffidence
Cypress	Death: Mourning

Daffodil	Regard
Dahlia	Instability
Daisy	Innocence
Daisy, Garden	I share your sentiments
Daisy, Michaelmas	Farewell
Daisy, Parti-coloured	Beauty
Daisy, Wild	I will think of it
Damask Rose	Brilliant complexion
Dandelion	Rustic oracle
Daphne odora	Painting the lily
Dead leaves	Sadness
Dianthus	Make haste
Deadly Nightshade	Falsehood
Dock	Patience
Dogsbane	Deceit : Falsehood
Dogwood	Durability
Dragon Plant	Snare
Dragonswort	Horror
Dried Flax	Utility

Ebony Tree	Blackness
Eglantine, Sweet-brier	Poetry: I wound to heal
Elder	Zealousness
Elm	Dignity
Enchanter's Nightshade	Witchcraft: Sorcery
Endive	Frugality
Eupatorium	Delay
Everflowering Candytuft	Indifference
Evergreen Clematis	Poverty
Evergreen Thorn	Solace in adversity
Everlasting	Never-ceasing remembrance
Everlasting Pea	Lasting pleasure

F

Fennel	Worthy of all praise
Fern	Fascination
Fig Tree	Prolific
Filbert	Reconciliation
Flax	I feel your kindness
Fleur-de-Lys	Flame: I burn
Flowering Reed	Confidence in heaven
Flower-of-an-Hour	Delicate beauty
Fly Orchis	Error
Fool's Parsley	Silliness
For-get-me-not	True love
Foxglove	Insincerity
Foxtail Grass	Sporting
French Honeysuckle	Rustic beauty
French Marigold	Jealousy
French Willow	Bravery & humanity
Fuchsia, Scarlet	Taste
Fuller's Teasel	Misanthropy
Fumitory	Spleen

G

Garden Anemone	Forsaken
Garden Chervil	Sincerity
Garden Daisy	I partake your sentiments
Garden Marigold	Uneasiness
Garden Ranunculus	You are rich in attractions
Garden Sage	Esteem
Garland of Roses	Reward of virtue
Germander Speedwell	Facility
Geranium, Dark	Melancholy
Geranium, Ivy	Bridal favour
Geranium, Lemon	Unexpected meeting
Geranium, Nutmeg	Expected meeting
Geranium Oak-leaved	True friendship
Geranium, Pencilled	Ingenuity
Geranium, Scarlet	Comforting

Germander Speedwell

Geranium Rose-scented	Preference
Geranium, Silver-leaved	Recall
Geranium, Wild	Steadfast piety
Gillyflower	Bonds of affection
Glory Flower	Glorious beauty
Goat's Rue	Reason
Golden Rod	Precaution
Gooseberry	Anticipation
Gourd	Extent: Bulk
Grape, Wild	Charity
Grass	Submission: Utility
Guelder Rose	Winter: Age

Harebell	Submission: Grief
Hawkweed	Quicksightedness
Hawthorn	Hope
Hazel	Reconciliation
Heath	Solitude
Helenium	Tears
Heliotrope	Devotion: Faithfulness
Hellebore	Scandal: Calumny
Helmet Flower	Knight-errantry
Hemlock	You will be my death
Hemp	Fate
Henbane	Imperfection
Hepatica	Confidence
Hibiscus	Delicate beauty
Holly	Foresight
Holy Herb	Enchantment
Hollyhock	Ambition: Fecundity
Honesty	Honesty: Fascination
Honey Flower	Love sweet & secret

Honeysuckle	Generous & devoted affection
Honeysuckle (Coral)	The colour of my fate
Honeysuckle (French)	Rustic beauty
Hop	Injustice
Hornbeam	Ornament
Horse Chestnut	Luxury
Hortensia	You are cold
Houseleek	Vivacity: Domestic industry
Houstonia	Content
Hoya	Sculpture
Humble Plant	Despondency
Hundred-leaved Rose	Dignity of mind
Hyacinth	Sport: Game: Play
Hyacinth, White	Unobtrusive loveliness
Hydrangea	A boaster: Heartlessness
Hyssop	Cleanliness

Ice Plant	Your looks freeze me
Indian Cress	Warlike trophy
Indian Jasmine (Ipomoea)	Attachment
Indian Pink (double)	Always lovely
Indian Plum	Privation
Iris	Message
Iris, German	Flame
Ivy	Fidelity: Marriage
Ivy, Sprig of with tendrils	Assiduous to please

Jacob's Ladder	Come down
Japan Rose	Beauty is your only attraction
Jasmine	Amiability
Jasmine, Cape	Transport of joy
Jasmine, Carolina	Separation
Jasmine, Indian	I attach myself to you
Jasmine, Yellow	Grace & elegance
Jonquil	I desire a return of affection
Juniper	Succour: Protection

Kennedia	Mental beauty
Kingcups	Desire of riches

Laburnum	Forsaken: Pensive beauty
Lady's Slipper	Capricious beauty
Lagerstraemia	Eloquence
Lantana	Rigour
Larch	Audacity: Boldness
Larkspur	Lightness: Levity
Larkspur, Pink	Fickleness
Larkspur, Purple	Haughtiness
Laurel	Glory
Laurel, Ground	Perseverance
Laurel, Mountain	Ambition
Laurel-leaved Magnolia	Dignity
Laurestina	A token
Lavender	Distrust
Lemon	Zest
Lemon Blossoms	Fidelity in love
Lilac, Field	Humility
Lilac, Purple	First emotions of love

Lilac, White	Youthful innocence
Lily, Day	Coquetry
Lily, Imperial	Majesty
Lily, White	Youthful innocence
Lily, Yellow	Falsehood : Gaity
Lily of the Valley	Return of happiness
Linden	Conjugal love
Live Oak	Liberty
Liverwort	Confidence
Lobelia	Malevolence
London Pride	Frivolity
Lotus	Eloquence
Lotus Flower	Estranged love
Love-in-a-Mist	Perplexity
Love-lies-bleeding	Hopeless not heartless
Lucern	Life
Lupin	Voraciousness : Imagination

Magnolia	Love of nature
Mallow	Mildness
Mallow, Marsh	Beneficence
Mallow, Venetian	Delicate beauty
Maple	Reserve
Marigold	Grief
Marigold, African	Vulgar minds
Marigold, French	Jealousy
Marjoram	Blushes
Marvel of Peru	Timidity
Meadow Lychnis	Wit
Meadow Saffron	My best days are past
Meadowsweet	Uselessness
Mercury	Goodness
Mesembryanthemum	Idleness
Mezereon	Desire to please
Michaelmas Daisy	Afterthought
Mignonette	Your qualities surpass your charms

Mossy
Saxifrage

Milkvetch	Your presence softens my pains
Mimosa	Sensitiveness
Mint	Virtue
Mistletoe	I surmount difficulties
Mock Orange	Counterfeit
Monkshood	A deadly foe is near
Monkshood	Chivalry-Knight-errantry
Moonwort	Forgetfulness
Morning Glory	Affectation
Moschatel	Weakness
Mossy Saxifrage	Affection
Mountain Ash	Prudence
Mouse-eared Chickweed	Ingenuous simplicity
Mulberry Tree	Wisdom
Musk Plant	Weakness
Mustard Seed	Indifference
Myrtle	Love

Mos- chatel

Narcissus	Egotism
Nasturtium	Patriotism
Nemophila	Success everywhere
Nettle. Stinging	You are spiteful
Nightblooming Cereus	Transient beauty

Oak Leaves	Bravery
Oats	Witching soul of music
Oleander	Beware
Olive	Peace
Orange Flowers	Chastity: Bridal festivities
Orchis	A belle
Osmunda	Dreams
Oxeye	Patience

Palm	Victory
Pansy	Thoughts
Parsley	Festivity
Pasque Flower	You have no claims
Passion Flower	Religious superstition
Patience Dock	Patience
Pea, Everlasting	An appointed meeting
	Lasting pleasure
Pea, Sweet	Departure
Peach	Your qualities like your
	charms are unequalled
Peach Blossom	I am your captive
Pear	Affection
Pennyroyal	Flee away
Peony	Shame: bashfulness
Peppermint	Warmth of feeling
Periwinkle, Blue	Early friendship
Periwinkle, White	Pleasures of memory
Pheasant's Eye	Remembrance

Phlox	Unanimity
Pimpernel	Change assignation
Pine-apple	You are perfect
Pine, Spruce	Hope in adversity
Pink	Boldness
Pink, Carnation	Woman's love
Pink, Indian (double)	Always lovely
Pink, Indian (single)	Aversion
Pink, Mountain	Aspiring
Pink, Red (double)	Pure & ardent love
Pink, Single	Pure love
Pink, Variegated	Refusal
Pink, White	Ingenuousness: Talent
Plane Tree	Genius
Plum Tree	Fidelity
Plum, Wild	Independence.
Polyanthus	Pride of riches
Polyanthus (crimson)	The heart's mystery
Polyanthus (lilac)	Confidence
Pomegranate	Foolishness

Pomegranate Flower	Mature elegance
Poplar, Black	Courage
Poplar, White	Time
Poppy, Red	Consolation
Poppy, Scarlet	Fantastic extravagance
Poppy, White	Sleep: My bane
Primrose	Early youth
Primrose, Evening	Inconstancy
Purple Clover	Provident
Pyrus japonica	Fairies' fire

Quaking Grass	Agitation
Quamoclit	Busybody
Queen's Rocket	You are the Queen of coquettes: Fashion
Quince	Temptation

Ragged Robin	Wit
Ranunculus	You are radiant with charms
Red Catchfly	Youthful love
Reed	Complaisance:Music
Rhubarb	Advice
Rocket	Rivalry
Rose	Love
Rose, Austrian	Thou art all that is lovely
Rose, Bridal	Happy love
Rose, Burgundy	Unconscious beauty
Rose, Cabbage	Ambassador of love
Rose, Campion	Only deserve my love
Rose, Carolina	Love is dangerous
Rose, China	Beauty always new
Rose, Christmas	Tranquillize my anxiety
Rose, Daily	Thy smile I aspire to
Rose, Damask	Brilliant complexion
Rose, Dog	Pleasure & pain
Rose, Guelder	Winter : Age
Rose, Hundred-leaved	Pride

Rose, Maiden Blush	If you love me you will find out
Rose, Multiflora	Grace
Rose, Mundi	Variety
Rose, Musk Cluster	Charming
Rose, Single	Simplicity
Rose, Thornless	Early attachment
Rose, Unique	Call me beautiful
Rose, White	I am worthy of you
Rose, full-bloom placed over two buds	Secrecy
Rose, White & Red together	Unity
Roses, Crown of	Reward of virtue
Rosebud, Red	Pure and lovely
Rosebud, White	Girlhood
Rosebud, Moss	Confession of love
Rosemary	Remembrance
Rudbeckia	Justice
Rue	Disdain
Rush	Docility

Saffron Crocus	Mirth
Saffron, Meadow	My happiest days are past
Sage	Domestic virtue
Saint John's Wort	Animosity: Superstition
Saxifrage, Mossy	Affection
Scabious	Unfortunate love
Scarlet Lychnis	Sunbeaming eyes
Sensitive Plant	Sensibility: Delicate feelings
Shamrock	Light-heartedness
Snapdragon	Presumption
Snowdrop	Hope
Sorrel	Affection
Sorrel, Wood	Joy
Southernwood	Jest: Bantering
Spanish Jasmine	Sensuality
Spearmint	Warmth of sentiment
Speedwell	Female fidelity
Speedwell Germander	Facility
Speedwell Spiked	Semblance
Spider Ophrys	Adroitness

Meadow Saffron

Spiked Willow Herb	Pretension
Spindle Tree	Your charms are engraven on my heart
Star of Bethlehem	Purity
Starwort	Afterthought
Starwort, American	Cheerfulness in old age
Stock	Lasting beauty
Stock, Ten Week	Promptness
Stonecrop	Tranquility
Strawberry Tree	Esteem & love
Sumach, Venice	Splendour Intellectual exercise
Sunflower, Dwarf	Adoration
Sunflower, Tall	Haughtiness
Sweet Basil	Good wishes
Sweetbrier	I wound to heal
Sweetbrier, Yellow	Decrease of love
Sweet Pea	Delicate pleasures
Sweet Sultan	Felicity
Sweet William	Gallantry
Syringa	Memory

Star of Bethlehem

Tamarisk	Crime
Tansy (Wild)	I declare War against you
Teasel	Misanthropy
Tendrils of Climbing Plants	Ties
Thistle, Common	Austerity
Thistle, Fullers	Misanthropy
Thistle, Scotch	Retaliation
Thorn Apple	Deceitful charms
Thorn, branch of	Severity
Thrift	Sympathy
Throatwort	Neglected beauty
Thyme	Activity
Tiger Flower	For once may pride befriend me
Traveller's Joy	Safety
Tree of Life	Old age
Trefoil	Revenge

Tremella Nestoc	Resistance
Trillium Pictum	Modest beauty
Truffle	Surprise
Trumpet Flower	Fame
Tuberose	Dangerous pleasures
Tulip	Fame
Tulip, Red	Declaration of love
Tulip, Variegated	Beautiful eyes
Tulip, Yellow	Hopeless love
Turnip	Charity
Tussilage (Sweet scented)	Justice shall be done to you

Ulex	Humility

Valerian	An accommodating disposition
Valerian, Greek	Rupture
Venice, Sumach	Intellectual elegance: Splendour
Venus' Car	Fly with me
Venus' Looking-glass	Flattery
Venus Trap	Deceit
Vernal Grass	Poor, but happy
Veronica	Fidelity
Vervain	Enchantment
Vine	Intoxication
Violet, Blue	Faithfulness
Violet, Dame	Watchfulness
Violet, Sweet	Modesty
Violet, Yellow	Rural happiness
Virginian Spiderwort	Momentary happiness
Virgin's Bower	Filial love
Volkamenia	May you be happy

W

Walnut	Intellect : Stratagem
Wall-flower	Fidelity in adversity
Water Lily	Purity of heart
Wheat Stalk	Riches
White Jasmine	Amiableness
White Lily	Purity & modesty
White Mullein	Good nature
White Pink	Talent
Whortleberry	Treason
Willow, Creeping	Love forsaken
Willow, French	Bravery & humanity
Willow, Water	Freedom
Willow Weeping	Mourning
Willow Herb	Pretension
Winter Cherry	Deception
Witch Hazel	A spell
Woodbine	Fraternal love
Wood Sorrel	Joy : Maternal tenderness
Wormwood	Absence

Xanthium	Rudeness: Pertinacity
Xeranthemum	Cheerfulness under adversity
Yew	Sorrow
Zephyr Flower	Expectation
Zinnia	Thoughts of absent friends

LINNAEUS'S DIAL OF FLOWERS

	opens	closes
Goat's Beard	3·00	9·00
Late-flowering Dandelion	4·00	12·00
Hawkweed Picris	4·00	12·00
Alpine Hawk's Beard	4·00	12·00
Wild Succory	4·00	12·00
Naked Stalked Poppy	5·00	7·00
Copper-coloured Day-Lily	5·00	7·00
Smooth Sowthistle	5·00	11·00
Blue-flowered Sowthistle	5·00	12·00
Field Bindweed	5·00	4·00
Spotted Cat's Ear	6·00	4·00
White Waterlily	7·00	5·00
Garden Lettuce	7·00	10·00
African Marigold	7·00	3·00
Mouse-ear Hawkweed	8·00	2·00
Proliferous Pink	8·00	1·00
Field Marigold	9·00	3·00
Purple Sandwort	9·00	2·00
Creeping Mallow	9·00	12·00
Chickweed	9·00	10·00

The time that flowers open

The time that flowers close

A VICTORIAN DIAL OF FLOWERS

	opens
Yellow Goatsbeard	3·00
Common Base Hawkweed	4·00
Bristly Helminthia	4·00
Alpine Borkhausia	4·00
Naked Stalked Poppy	5·00
Orange Day Lily	5·00
Red Hawkweed	5·00
Common Nipplewort	5·00
Meadow Goshmore	6·00
Red Base Hawkweed	6·00
White Waterlily	7·00
White Spiderwort	7·00
Garden Lettuce	7·00
Common Pimpernel	7·00
Mouse-eared Hawkweed	8·00
Field Marigold	9·00
Purple Sandwort	9·00
Ice Plant	10·00
Red Sandwort	10·00

	closes
Bristly Helminthia	12·00
Alpine Agathyrsus	12·00
Creeping Mallow	12·00
Red Pink	1 ·00
Red Boxhawkweed	1 · 00
Bearded Mesembryanthemum	2 ·00
Small Purslane	2 · 00
Field Marigold	3 · 00
African Marigold	3 · 00
Ice Plant	4· 00
White Spiderwort	4·00
Meadow Goshmore	5 · 00
Waterlily	6 · 00
Naked Stalked Poppy	7· 00
Copper-coloured Day Lily	7· 00
Common Dandelion	8 ·00
Yellow Goatsbeard	9 · 00
Garden Lettuce	10·00
Common Sowthistle	11·00

CHINESE CALENDAR OF FLOWERS

JANUARY	Plum Blossom
FEBRUARY	Peach Blossom
MARCH	Tree Peony
APRIL	Cherry Blossom
MAY	Magnolia

JUNE	Pomegranate
JULY	Lotus
AUGUST	Pear Blossom
SEPTEMBER	Mallow
OCTOBER	Chrysanthemum
NOVEMBER	Gardenia
DECEMBER	Poppy

JAPANESE CALENDAR OF FLOWERS

JANUARY	Pine
FEBRUARY	Plum
MARCH	Peach
APRIL	Cherry
MAY	Iris

JUNE   Wistaria
JULY   Morning Glory
AUGUST   Lotus
SEPTEMBER   Chrysanthemum
OCTOBER   Autumn Nanakusa
NOVEMBER   Maple
DECEMBER   Bamboo